Left

Without

A

Warning

MARQUESSA PRATER

DEDICATION

This book is dedicated to all My Heavenly Angels, to the ones that grieving, suffer from depression. Remember The Lord himself goes before you and will be with you; he will never leave you nor forsake you. Do not be afraid; do not be discouraged."
Deuteronomy 31:8 NIV

Table of Contents

ACKNOWLEDGMENTS

"I would like to express my special thanks of gratitude to Former Teachers from grade school. "Who encouraged me to write a book Wow! "This is my third book I have published. "I'm truly grateful for you all. "So many saw something in me that I didn't see in myself. "Now my gift will be shared worldwide. "I would also like to thank The Designer of my book cover, Photographer Makeup Artist and to everyone that has purchase my books Thank You!

- Much Love

– Marquessa Prater

Chapter One

"THREE'S COMPANY"

O kay! Ms. Oakwood you and your precious baby boy are ready to be discharged. "Do you need me to call Transportation Service for you? "No thank you my Fiancé is downstairs in the Cafeteria. "I will let him know.

[Nurse Sharon] Okay! "I will contact Patient Transport to take you and your son downstairs. "Would you like a car seat and formula?

[Tesla] "No thank you he has more than enough stuff.

[Nurse Sharon] "Well I wish you a wonderful journey for you and your precious baby boy take care.

[Tesla] "I definitely will and thank you for everything.

[Nurse Sharon] "It's our pleasure to treat our patients with great hospitality.

Hey Baby! You can go ahead and get the car and meet us at the Main Entrance. "Patient Transport is here to bring us down stairs. "Yes! "I'm on my way" "As we were headed home. Tears started to descend down my face. "Of course, they were tears of joy but I was missing my father. "I can see him now fighting who's going to hold Rayquan first.

[Rayquan] Why are you crying Tesla?

[Tesla] "Just missing My Dad.

[Rayquan] "Baby don't cry I miss him too. This is hard on me as well "You having a deceased father and I have deceased parents. "Just know I got us forever. There will be many days we reminisce but our memories will last a life time. Our son will know about his grandparents. "We will get through this together.

[Tesla] "Thank you for always being so loving and supportive I truly appreciate you.

[Rayquan] "Anytime baby!

[Tesla] As we arrived home there was a Congratulations Banner in the yard and balloons. Wow Baby! "This is so nice you never seem to amaze me." "As I open the door and walk inside. Our living room was full with gifts, balloons. "There was prepared lunch and desserts simply amazing. Baby how did you find the time to do all this?

[Rayquan] "Don't worry about that I told you I got my Queen and Prince.

[Tesla] "Son mommy couldn't have chosen a better Father for you.

Chapter Two

Mama's Love

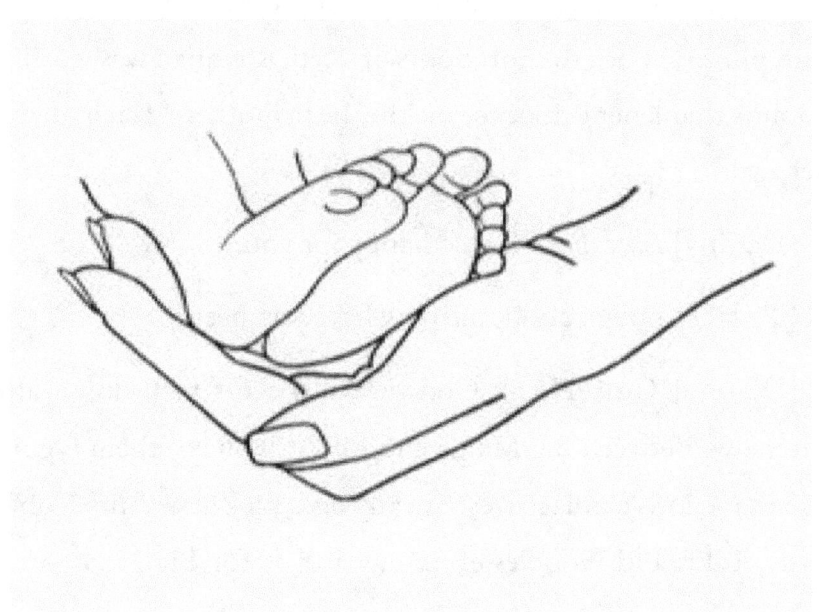

Girl why is you Face Timing me at 8:00 AM?

[Destiny] "I'm not calling for you "I want to see my nephew. [Tesla] "What you not going to do is work my nerves. [Destiny] Bitch Please! Let me see my nephew. Damn!!!! Tesla what have you been feeding him? "He almost ready for football" I know he's not going to be able to fit the outfits I bought him. [Tesla] "Girl your ass is crazy my baby love to eat and you know what they say. "The key to a man's heart is a home cooked meal. "Well his is mommy milkshake bottle. [Destiny] "He is so freaking handsome Tesla How are you adjusting to motherhood? [Tesla] "Destiny I still can't believe I'm a mother now from the 17hrs of labor, changing diapers, making bottles seem like every hour, photo shoots, to short hours of sleep. Rayquan was worth it. Mommy thank her Prince for making her a mother. "I'm in love all over again."

[Destiny] Awe Tesla I'm so happy for you.

[Tesla] "Enough about me how have you been?

[Destiny] Girl! Thank God we will be off lock down after tomorrow. Between Big Mama and Lil Zack one of them is going to send me into cardiac arrest at early age. Lil Zack wants Roblox Cards, Takis and Noodles every day and as for Big Mama every time I walk out the door. "Don't forget your mask & hand sanitizer and I'm just sitting on the porch or running across the street to the store. Tesla they been stressing me out. "Tomorrow is actually the same day Big Dot Grandma passed away. "So I figured instead her staying home being down. "I know she likes Amusement Parks. So we are go to Magical Fun Spot. " [Tesla] "Destiny your behind is crazy less than 24hrs you will be free and that was very thoughtful of you to cheer Big Dot up. "I know that she would really appreciate that. "I definitely know how Big Dot feels. The other week when we were on our way from the Hospital. "I got emotional because I was missing my dad. "This is when I need him the most. "Don't get me wrong I'm very thankful for a wonder Fiancé but there's nothing like the love my daddy had for me. [Destiny] "Tesla, I know it's hard you gain a Guardian Angel who has the best view. "You are a great friend and even better mother. "Losing a parent is tough I had to be the mom and dad to Lil Zack at such a young age. Hell, I didn't know who to turn to. "I didn't have any older siblings where I can turn to them for advice. "Until I found you and Cha-Cha. "You both have showed me genuine love. "I thought these men love me because how they tip me at Tasty's, put food in my house and shower me with gifts. No, they just wanted the pocket book and not the one you carry on your shoulder. Big Dot gives me the love I been missing. "She never try to buy me for sex or throw up what she does for me. " She communicates with me without verbally abusing me. [Tesla] Destiny! "That's what real friends are for." The same way you are here for me. "I will be here for you" "We are no longer friends" We are sisters for life.

Chapter Three

"YOU'RE safe with me"

[Intercom] Attention! "All Patrons thank you for visiting Magical Fun Spot "Please remove all items out your pockets and place them in the grey trays and proceed through the Metal Detectors . "No outside food or drinks are allowed on premises. "We hope your visit is a Magical Experience. "Stay hydrated and have magical fun.

[Ticket Agent] Hello! Welcome to the Magical Fun Spot. "How many tickets will you be purchasing today?

[Destiny] "May I have two Adult Tickets?

[Ticket Agent] Certainly, that will be $24.00 out of $30.00. Okay Madam! $6.00 is your change. "Please enjoy your day.

[Destiny] "Thank you we surely will"

[Photographer:] Hello! Welcome to Magical Fun Spot. "Would you like to take a photo?

[Big Dot] "Yes come on Bae

[Photographer] 1...2...3 "Here is your ticket be sure to look at your photo on your way out.

[Big Dot] Thank you!

[Destiny] "I can't wait for a corn dog, cotton candy, chicken on stick, roasted corn.

[Big Dot] OMG! "Bae you have an appetite huh?

[Destiny] "Yes Bae my shy days are over with you. "I made sure I didn't eat anything before I came.

[Big Dot] "Thank you Bae for getting me out the house this means a lot. "My Grandma was everything to me.

[Destiny]" No need to thank me" I know you would do the same for me.

[Big Dot] "Let's get on the Triple Decker"

[Destiny] "Oh, Hell No! "Look how high that goes.

[Big Dot] "Come on I got you I won't let anything happen to you."

[Ride Attendant] "Please hold on and stay seated to rides stops.

[Destiny] "I can't believe I'm on this. "I'm afraid of heights.

[Big Dot] "Don't be it's time to face your fears.

[Destiny] Dear God; "Please don't let this be my last day on earth. "I still got to watch over Lil Zack and Big Mama.

[Big Dot laughing] Relax Bae "This ride will be over before you know it. "See Bae you did great. "I'm proud of you.

[Tesla] "I will stick to the Merry Go Round. "Let's go eat and play some games. "I will have to warm up for the next roller coaster. "This food was banging. [Big Dot] "Destiny you are so funny and caring. Out of all my girlfriends I've had. "You are the only one that cares about my feelings and not just my pockets. [Destiny]Awe baby the feelings are mutual. "You have showed me so much in the time we have been dating. "That I shouldn't be so quick to prejudge. "You show me the definition of love not just physical but mentally and emotionally thank you. "I'm happy with you and happy I was able to put a smile on your face. "Now come on so I can whoop your ass in these games. [Big Dot] "Okay bet look check this out when you lose make sure you are ready to ride the Thunder.

[Destiny] "PLEASE DON'T LET ME LOOSE.

Chapter Four

"RESPECT My Business"

Our staff are there to help.

Please be patient and respect our staff.

THANK YOU

ZERO TOLERANCE

PLEASE RESPECT OUR STAFF

[L a'kisha] "All that talking you doing holding up time. "Cut and less talking. [Rayquan] La'kisha! "You can always leave if you have somewhere to be.

[La'lisha] "Oh, so you going to throw me and your son out?

[Rayquan] "La'kisha let's not do this in front of Customers. [La'kisha] "I can say what I want when I want. "You think you are a big stepper now because you got this shop. With you snitching ass how the hell you get a shop and just was released from jail?

[Rayquan] "Again, La'kisha this is not the place. "Either respect my business or leave.

[La'kisha] "I'm not going anywhere until you start doing for your son.

[Rayquan] Look La'Kisha! "I tried to be nice this is my shop take your delusional, disrespectful ass up on out of here. "Go find your son father because I'm not the one. You already received your test results just like I did & I'm 99% not his father. "You wanted attention now there you have it.

[La'kisha] "I hope this bitch burn down you dog ass nigga.

[Rayquan] Bye La'kisha!

[La'kisha] "Yeah watch your back.

[Rayquan] "Keep on with the threats your ass going to be right in jail. "I would cool it if I was you. "Your son already doesn't have a father and next not a mother. "Don't have in the system for your foolishness.

[La'kisha] "Fuck you Rayquan.

[Rayquan] "I apologize everyone that you had to witness me step out of character. [Customers] "It's all good Quan you hold your composure for a long time. "She had it coming" I appreciate everyone for understanding.

[Phone Rings] Thank you for calling Dollar Cuts "Rayquan speaking how may help you?

[Beep...Beep...]

[Rayquan] "I guess they had the wrong number. What a day! "Let me clean up and head home.

[Door Opens] "Can I get a clean-up by the first time father before you close?

[Rayquan] "What's up Dwayne? [Walks to Rayquan and gives handshake]

[Dwayne] "So how is it as a father now?

[Rayquan] "Man Wayne my son has gave me my second chance of life. "Every day I open my eyes. "I think about making wise decisions. "I won't let him make the decisions I've made I'm going to try my best to be that father, mentor my son needs. How is everything being with you?

[Dwayne] "Everything good the shop won $10,000 at Lil Wave Car Show. "We had that Camouflage Wet Paint on them Box Chevy's. "Chastity and I are still together. "I know she's the one I might have to pop that question soon. [Rayquan] "Now that's what's up I'm happy for you. [Dwayne] Thanks Man! "Look check in with wifey and let's go have some drinks. [Rayquan] "You got jokes man here the mirror you done. [Dwayne] Oh Yeah! You got a nigga looking Red Carpet in this bitch. Now about those drinks? [Rayquan] "Hold up!

"Hey baby I'm about to go have some drinks with Dwayne are you and Jr okay?

[Tesla] "Yes we are fine and okay be safe. " I love you"

[Rayquan] "I love you too. "Alright let's go!

Chapter Five

"Unexpected Guest"

[Server Rachel] "Welcome to Big Moe's I'm your Server Rachel. "So what brings you in today?

[Dwayne] "We are celebrating my good friend! " Rayquan as a new father.

[Server Rachel] "Oh Wow! Congratulations this is definitely a celebration. "I'm a mother of three and I can't imagine life without them.

[Rayquan] Thank you! "Yes my son is one of my biggest blessings.

[Dwayne] Rachel can we have a couple of shots of Hennessy and Patron?

[Server Rachel] Certainly any appetizers?

[Rayquan] Hot Wings with blue cheese

[Dwayne] Chicken Sliders

[Server Rachel] "I will put in your order.

[Rayquan] "Man this place is nice"

[Dwayne] "You know Dollar own this right?

[Rayquan] Nawl!

[Dwayne] Yeah Dollar invested his money in a lot of Properties in Tampa. He will always going to be a Living Legend.

[Rayquan] "Always" Hold up! "Let me take this call Hello!

[Beep. Beep]

[Dwayne] Everything good?

[Rayquan] Yeah!

[Server Rachel] Okay Gentlemen! "Here are your shots and appetizers enjoy!

[Thank You]

[Dwayne] Aye Quan do you mind if my homeboy join us? "He just got in town"

[Rayquan] "No I don't mind at all."

[Dwayne] "Ok bet! "Let me tell him to meet me here.

[Rayquan] "Aye Wayne I'll be back got to go take a leak. As I started walking back to the table. "From far away Dwayne homeboy was built like Dollar. As I was an inch to the table. Dwayne homeboy turn around.

[Unexpected Guest] "I heard there's a new father in town?

[Rayquan] "What the HELL! " Dwayne homeboy was Dollar.

[Dollar] "So you going to stand there and cry or show a nigga some love?

[Rayquan] "Awe Man! [Hugs Dollar]

[Dollar] "I see you kept your word and did what I asked for you to do. " I know you like how I'm seating next to you and I suppose to be 6ft under. "A lot of unanswered questions are running through your head. " It's was a purpose I fake my own deaf to get myself right. "I paid the hospital and funeral home a good penny to keep quiet. " I knew the only way to get myself together and take things seriously was to leave. "So I escape on my private jet and stated in my home in Columbia. "I check in periodically with Dwayne to see how everything was going. "I had a live in Medical Team to help me with my addition with Substance Abuse. " I knew if I stayed in my familiar environment. "I wouldn't never stop" I missed out on a lot but gain more knowledge. Dwayne video tape Tesla Graduation and Graduation Party with a hidden camera. "I witnessed the special moments. "Just wasn't in everyone presence. "Oh and you handle the delivery quiet well I saw that too. "I'm done with drinking completely & all my operations have been passed to Locals. "My focus is to continue to have successful properties get involved in youth and drug addiction programs. "My family is my number one priority. "I want to be that grandpa that gives my grandchild everything. Watch him at every school plays, award ceremony, and basketball and football games. "With a camcorder shouting that's my grandson. "I guess now you realize who been calling you anonymous. Quan whatever you do "DON'T MENTION THIS TESLA "

[Rayquan] Man! "I'm lost for words right now you been gone at some of the hardest times and you expect me to quiet. I've been the one there to comfort Tesla to wipe her tears, pray with her. "Yes it's my job to protect my family but the time she needed her father's love. " I couldn't fulfil for her. "Don't get me wrong I'm ecstatic to see you but this a lot to keep away from my soon to be wife.

[Dollar] "Quan I respect your response and you absolutely right I have missed out and there's no excuse I can I give but I can insure you I'm here to stay. "Let me handle this give me your word you won't say anything. [Rayquan] "No I won't it's not my place to do so it's yours. [Rayquan stands up from the table. "To shake Dollar and Dwayne hand and walks off]

Chapter Six

"Keeping Secrets from MY FIANCÉ"

[R]ayquan] "God I know that you don't make any mistakes but if I never agreed to go have drinks with Dwayne. "I wouldn't be in this situation. "Here I go again in another situation that I had no business being in. "How do I keep a straight face when I walk in the house? How can I not tell Tesla her father is still alive? How is this being a faithful? "Man I was better off not coming home. "I feel like I'm cheating on my Fiancé. "I get where Dollar is coming from but this is one I wish I opt on. "Don't get me after all Dollar did for me I guess this is my way of repaying him. "I wouldn't be the man, father, boss and fiancé I am today. Then its Tesla the mother of my child, best friend, and soon to be my wife. That I holding a lie from. "Before I go in the house let me save Dollar number as Donald. "Just in case Tesla see an incoming call or Text because if she see Dollar Name. "Who knows what would happen". This definitely isn't the night I want to find the out. "I pray they are sleep when I walk in the house. [Tesla] "Hey baby did you enjoy yourself? [Rayquan damn,] "Hey Baby I wasn't expecting you to be up. " I know you usually be sleep by now." To answer your question. "Yes I did. How was your day?

[Tesla] "That's good I'm happy you enjoyed yourself. "My day was good until I dose off and had the weirdest dream about my dad. "He knock on the door with lots of gifts and said hey baby girl. [Reach in with his arms open and gave me hug and kiss on the cheek and said "Where is my grand baby?] "Felt so real & then I woke up and couldn't go back to sleep. [Rayquan] "You know Dollar will always be here in spirit. " Let me go run you a hot bubble bath. "I need for you to relax. [Tesla] "This is why I love you! [As she walk over and place her arms around Rayquan's neck embracing him with a kiss].

[Rayquan] "Let's go upstairs and get you your bath. " While Tesla was taking a relaxing bath. "I sat on the bed [lean my head over Jr in his bassinet.]

[Rayquan] "Jr you have the slightness idea what your Father been through today. " I guess I don't have to tell you about your grandfather when you get older. "He will be here to tell you himself. [Goodnight son daddy loves you.]

[Notification chimes] "I love you my boy thanks for all you have done for our family. "It's a lot to take in all at once. "I will take care of everything soon. "Kiss my baby girl and grandson for me.

Chapter Seven

"IT'S not you it's me!

[D]wayne] "Chastity you hardly said anything since I got here.

You're brief when I ask you questions, you gave me a church hug, and you didn't eat the food I brought you and now you sitting far from me. What is the problem?

[Chastity] "I think we should end this relationship. [Dwayne] "We are not ending anything. "I found who I want to continue my life with and that's with you and Star.

"Chastity you are so caught up who has walk out your life that you don't realize the man that you have been praying for is right in front of you.

[Chastity] Dwayne! I've been through a lot with Star's Father. "I know how it goes. " You start off the man I always dream of. "Then here comes the toxic arguments, coming in the midnight hours, ghost all calls or text messages. I'm tired of getting hurt by love. "The moment I start to love someone. "They show me why I shouldn't." It's not just about me it's about my daughter too. "We are a package deal and now that her father has passed away. " I have to be extra cautious of who I introduced her to. [Dwayne] "Look at me Chastity have I argue with you once? No

Haven't I answer your calls and texts? Yes

Have I been there for you and Star? Yes

"So all the things you are afraid of." I just asked you the questions back and you answer them accurately. Chastity, "I'm not your past I want to be your future."

I love you and Star. "I would never replace Star's father from her but I promise to accept her like my own. "I've been hurt before too but it would be unfair to treat you like the ones that hurt me right? Yes

So don't treat me like the men in your past. "This conversation is deceased and will not to be brought up anymore. " Now what movie did you pick for us to watch tonight?

[Chastity] Dairy of a Mad Black Woman

[Dwayne laughing] "Oh yeah you was definitely in your feelings. "Just the other night you was feeling all Jason Lyric and shit. [Chastity] "Whatever Dwayne! " Let me go warm up my food. [Dwayne] "See all you wanted was my attention acting stubborn about to starve yourself. [Chastity] Man! Start the movie.

[Dwayne] "It already stared its call "Chastity Wants My Attention [Actress are Chastity and Dwayne]

Chapter Eight

"See me after class"

[M]ercedes] "Mr. Butler you wanted to see me?

[Mr. Butler] Ms. Oakwood! "The purpose why I wanted to meet with you after class. "Your last two test scores have been below average. "This is unlike you is everything okay?

[Mercedes] "No everything is not Mr. Butler: "I've been trying to cope with my father's death. "My parents were my biggest supporters. "Now I don't feel like I have a team anymore. "My baby sister has move out and now has a family of her own. "Don't get me wrong I 'm very happy for her but I'm the one that supposed to move out and stared a family first. Instead I'm stuck in this big mansion. "Looking after my mother. "I'm afraid she might harm herself or commit suicide. "I don't know how to live or love anymore. "Since my dad and boyfriend passed away." "I'm afraid if I begin to love again. " I would go into this big depression like I am now if I lose someone again. "It's hard trying to stay focused with only 2hrs of sleep, constantly thinking about my mom and that I will receive a disturbing phone call that she was found dead. Mr. Butler! "I'm tired of going to sleep with a broken heart, People tell me it's going to be okay. How do they know? "On top of that today is my deceased boyfriend's birthday. [Mr. Butler] Wow! Mercedes I'm sorry you been going through that. "I know something was going on but wasn't expecting all this from you. " You are one of my straight A Students and I would hate to fail you. "I have spoken to some of the Administrators here and we think its best that you take some time away from school and join us back in the fall. [Free of charge] " Ms. Oakwood you doing your best. "Never feel that you're failure. Mercedes, "I know a young man that story is similar to yours. Here is his book this will be your final assignment and you can tell me your thoughts about the book. "When you return in the fall.

[Mercedes] Mr. Butler you are an Author? "That's amazing" [Mr. Butler] Yes Mercedes! "I see a lot in you that I once lost in myself. " My book will help you in your grieving process. "It's a short read so you will be able to finish it by tonight. "In the back of the book there's blank pages. "I want you write and cast all your thoughts and leave them there. "Then give it someone you trust. "Here's my business card call me anytime. "I will be praying for you and your family. "Mercedes it's going to be alright I believe in you.

[Mercedes] "As I come to the conclusion of Mr. Butler Book. "I'm appalled "Tonight I would let go of all my hurt in this book and start refresh in the morning.

Chapter Nine

"911, WHAT'S
YOUR EMERGENCY?

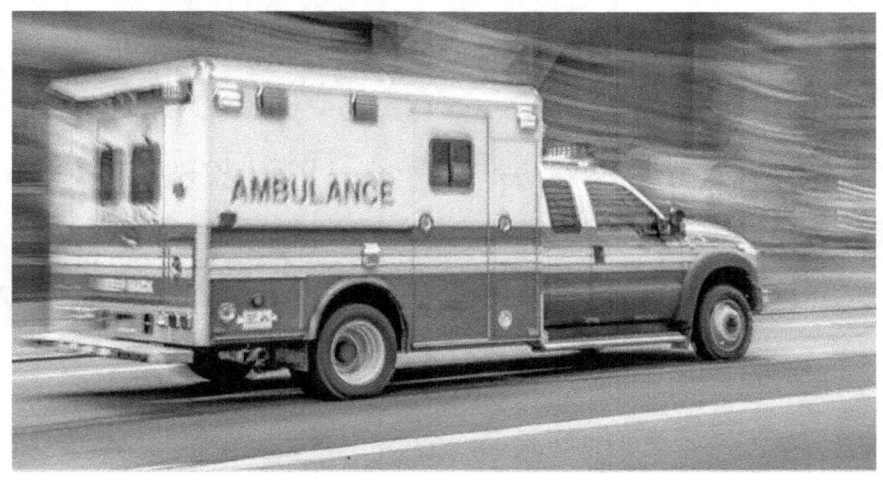

[T]esla] "I can't wait to see sissy for our sister time today.

"Normally it would be Mama, Cedes and I but Auntie

Jesse came and picked Mama for a Women's

Conference in Miami. "They should be back sometime later today. "Mama Face Time me yesterday from The Conference. "To see all the women loving on Mama made my heart smile. "Rayquan watching the baby so mommy can have some girl's time. Man! "Mercedes is not even answering the phone. "She probably still sleep or in the shower. OMG! "I will be waiting another hour until she's ready. "Cedes moves like a turtle" Let me head over there.

[Tesla opens the door]

Mercedes Oakwood!!! "I know you hear me calling you. " I'm coming up there wake your butt up. [Tesla stomping upstairs] "I know you hear me" [Tesla slams the door open standing in Mercedes door way. Girl wake up "I'm hungry Mercedes!!!! As I'm moving her arm back and forward I feel no pulse. "Mercedes stop playing now this nothing to joke about. "I began to perform CPR still no pulse.

[911 Dispatcher] 911, what's your emergency?

[Tesla] "My sister isn't breathing"

[911 Dispatcher] Are there any minors or any other adults in your home?

[Tesla] "No just my sister and I.

[911 Dispatcher] "Try to stay calm help is on the way."

[Tesla] As the Paramedics arrive and begin to perform CPR. "Mercedes [Mercedes still wasn't responding] as they put Mercedes on the stretcher and rush to the hospital. "I started to panic. [Running downstairs hands shaking while calling mama]

[Tesla] Mama! "Cedes, wasn't breathing when I arrive here she been rush to the hospital. "I'm behind the ambulance. [Diamond] No! "My baby Jesus help me right now. Tesla "I'm on my way"

[Tesla] As I get out the car and sit in the lobby I'm a nervous rack. I think about the time we was praying for daddy in this same lobby. Father God; "I can't have this to happen to me again.

[Diamond] Tesla! [Pacing to Tesla in the lobby]

[Tesla] "Mama I'm so happy you are here [Tesla hugs her mother].

[Diamond] Have you heard anything?

[Tesla] No Ma'am. Mama there is Mercedes Doctor.

[Doctor Wells] Hi Mrs. Oakwood! "We did all we could do and I'm sorry to inform you that Mercedes is no longer with us. "My condolences are with you and your family.

[Diamond] NO!!!!! "Not my baby "No, no, no [crying]

[Tesla] "I stood in the hallway watching the doctor walk away in anger and disbelief.

Why My Sister? "Mercedes was my best friend, my diary. "Cedes told me she would always be here. "If I didn't have my baby. "I would ask God to take me with her." My heart is no longer a shape it's broken into pieces. "As days went by still no calls or text messages from Cedes. " Today I have to face reality Cedes isn't coming back. "I question why she passed at such a young age. "We had so much plans from trips, my wedding and opening up our own food truck. "I won't question where her new home is. "I know she safely made it to Heaven. "I just wish it wasn't so sudden. Cedes look like the princess she truly was I asked God to get me through the letter I wrote to her.

Chapter Ten

"Letter to my sister"

[T]esla] "Praise the Lord everyone my name is Tesla Oakwood. " I'm Mercedes Sister thank you all for coming today. I have something I wrote to my sister.

Dear; Sis "Never would have thought God would call you home so soon.

Cedes it broke our hearts to lose you, but you did not go alone.

"You left us beautiful memories so we won't never be alone. We once was four now we're two you're in Heaven with Daddy now. "Lord knows we miss you and daddy too. Its hurts that you won't see your nephew grow. We had so much to see in this crazy world but you in Heaven now and always be my favorite girl. "I love you always your baby sister Tesla. [Audience stood up clapping]

As the Usher walk me back to my seat. Bishop Wright asked if anyone would like to say another Eulogy.

[I do] "A man shouted walking from the back of the church. I couldn't really see him. As he got closer it was my daddy. "Everyone mouth was wide open including mines." [Shock]

"I can hear the audience whispering to one another. "I thought he was dead. As My Father walk to the Altar. "I looked at Mama then to my left at Rayquan.

[Dollar] "Praise the Lord Everyone" "Yes it's me Bernie Oakwood and some may call me Dollar. I could stand here for hour's answer everyone questions but this is my princess time. "A

Princess is supposed to be protected by her King, treated with Royalty and I fail my Princess. Instead I was too selfish with my own life of no self-control of substance abuse. "I lost time with my family and didn't know the affects in had caused on my children and wife. I fake my own deaf to get myself right. So I would be appropriate to live in my household with the ladies of my life. There's no excuses of my behavior. Mercedes was the first to make me a Father and I wasn't the right Role Model but she was. Mercedes taught me leadership, responsibility, continuing education and love. Mercedes will always be daddy princess.

[Tesla] As daddy walked off stage. "He walk to Mercedes Casket to say his final farewell. "Daddy was truly hurt as stared at Mercedes. His legs and hands shaking. As he lean over Mercedes Casket crying to give Mercedes her final kiss. Bishop walk over placing a sheet over daddy back as he prayed for him at the Altar. "Bishop began to pray over daddy. Mama and the attire audience started moving their way towards the Altar [praying and worship together.] Jesus was really in the house of Lord. "We didn't just have a funeral we had church. "I question why daddy did what he did but to be honest he couldn't come at a better time. After we sent Mercedes off we arrive back home for her Repast with family and friends. [Dollar] "I miss you baby girl "daddy is here to stay. " I'm sorry for what has happen. I'm very proud of the woman and mother you have become. "Never question if I didn't care because I did that's why I left to get myself clean. " I love you always"

[Tesla]" I love you too daddy and I'm happy you're home. [Hugs and kiss her father] "I have someone I like for you to meet. [Tesla walks over to get Rayquan out his basinet]

[Dollar] "I'm a granddaddy [crying] Tesla he is so handsome look at that "You got your granddaddy nose and eyes. "Oh yeah he definitely an Oakwood [laughing] Hey man! "I'm your granddaddy [rock and kissing him in his arms] "[Tesla] While everyone was downstairs. "I went up to Mercedes room looking at her stuff smelling her favorite perfume, looking at her photo albums.

["I'm going to miss you sis]

"I started making up Cedes bed "she would hate that she left her bed like this. [Laughing]

To: Tesla [What's this?]

Hey Tesla! Before you read this book just know I love you and this will help you in your grieving process. "Don't worry about me I'm heal and better. " I'm proud of you and will forever be with you. "When you walking just remember "I'm always with you with the locket I brought you for graduation, when you need someone to talk to I added more pages. " So you can tell me your thoughts. [I'm always listen] "Still open up our food truck and stay out my room girl I know you being nosey love you sis Cedes!

Book Cast Members

Bernie A.K.A. Dollar (The Father)

Diamond (The Mother)

Mercedes (Sister)

Tesla (Daughter & Main Character)

RAYQUAN (Tesla FIANCÉ)

Rayquan Jr (Tesla son)

Cha-Cha & Destiny (Tesla Best Friends)

Star (Cha-Cha Daughter)

Big Dot (Destiny Girlfriend)

Dwayne (Tesla Cousin & CHA-Cha)

Big Mama (Destiny Grandmother)

Lil Zack (Destiny Brother)

La'Kisha (Rayquan Ex-Girlfriend)

Mr.Butler (Mercedes Teacher)

Jesse (Diamond Sister)

Dr.Wells (doctor)

Bishop (Bishop Wright)